Namaste
IS A GREETING

Suma Subramaniam

illustrated by Sandhya Prabhat

CANDLEWICK PRESS

Namaste is
a greeting.

A celebration.

Namaste is
"I bow to you."

A yoga pose.

A practice.

Silence.

Namaste is
loving the world.

Namaste is hello!

Sain baina uu!

BONJOUR!

ALOHA!

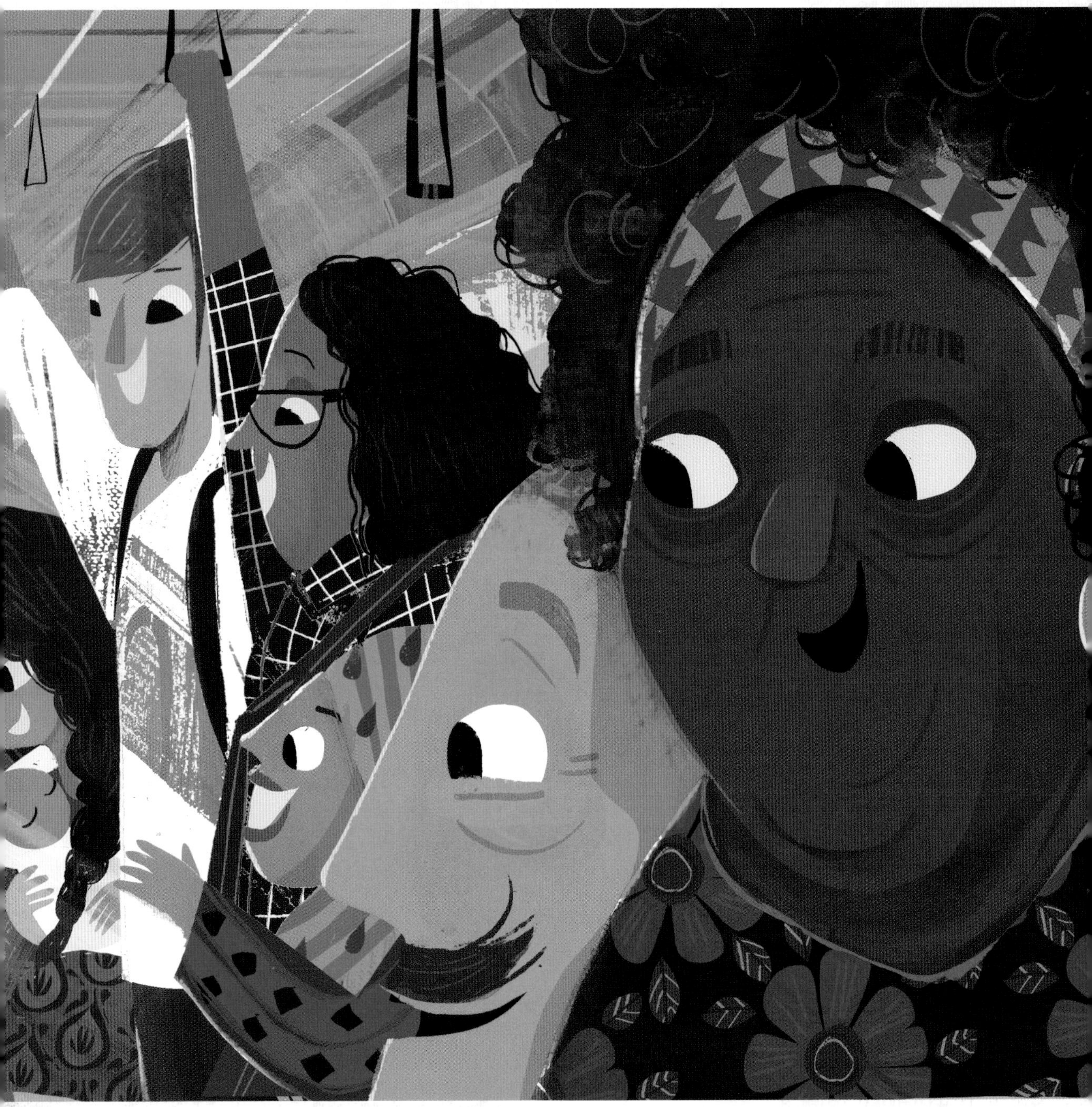

SALAAM!

Konnichiwa!

Jambo!

¡HOLA!

Namaste is joining
your palms together.

Say namaste when you're happy

or when you're feeling low.

Namaste
calms your heart
when things aren't
going right.

Namaste is saying
"You matter."

Namaste is peace.

It's a light,
a path
when the road
is unclear.

Say namaste and be still.

Or do something nice.

Offer namaste to heal
and comfort.

Namaste is the divine
in me honoring
the divine in you.

To Amma, Appa, and to children everywhere, namaste
SS

Dedicated to a time when we could talk, mingle,
and laugh freely, unmasked and unafraid, and to a
future where we can once again be that way
SP

Text copyright © 2022 by Suma Subramaniam
Illustrations copyright © 2022 by Sandhya Prabhat

First edition 2022

Library of Congress Catalog Card Number 2021953467
ISBN 978-1-5362-1783-4

22 23 24 25 26 27 CCP 10 9 8 7 6 5 4 3 2 1

Printed in Shenzhen, Guangdong, China

This book was typeset in Halewyn.
The illustrations were created digitally.

Candlewick Press
99 Dover Street
Somerville, Massachusetts 02144

www.candlewick.com